life in a bag

baljit ghuman

ISBN: 9781541330146
ISBN-13: 9781541330146

DEDICATION

For my teacher who acknowledged me for me,
Late. Mrs. Sawraj Kaur Bhinder.

Cover painting Ria K. Ghuman

ACKNOWLEDGMENTS

My gratitude to all those who have encouraged me to write.

There is nothing more satisfying for a writer to see his art appreciated.

Thank you!

www.baljitghuman.com

Don't be so giving
That you give away
All the love you had.

Keep a little
For yourself.

When the Kings are dead and the Kingdoms are gone, it is the rebels who shine through the history.

Yesterday,
was rough.

Today,
Is better.

Tomorrow,
Will be even better.

Keep hope.

I have always
Honoured my inner child.

He gives me my
Imagination,
My curiosity and
My determination
To try new things in life.

Without him
I will be soulless.

-B.G.

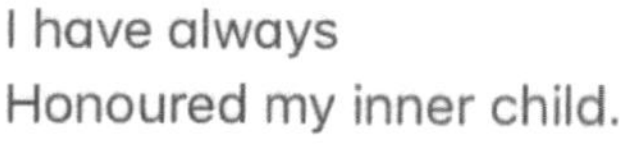

Life in a bag

No need to worry
If I would survive,
Be worry free about me.
I have learned to live without love.

It no longer matters:

If you pushed me away
Or pulled me close.
If you loved me
Or you hated me.
If you healed me
Or you hurt me.

You were part of my journey
You are part of my story.

Life in a bag

When I fall down
I will rise, I will stand.

I am a fighter
I will fight,
It is in me by design, by blood.

I have the
Midas touch.
Be cautious,
I may turn you
Into a poem.

Bruised, broken and rejected
I sit in calmness
Across the green fields
Gazing far into the flower bed.

The most beautiful
Of the flowers I see
Is the yellow weed flower
Staring out of the grass
With brightest of its colour

The yellow weed flower
Is still a flower
But alone
Bruised, broken and rejected.

–B.G.

Do yourself a favour.
Give yourself the permission to fail,
that is the only way out.

Polish your flaws
Wear your wounds;
As your badge of honour.

Carry on the battle.

You have burned me,
But I will rise from the ashes
Just like the Phoenix.

Renewed and youthful
I will return
To finish what you started.

Not for a moment think
That I am gone.

Revolution is not a storm
It's an ignited fire, a spark.

Revolution is not
Waiting for iron to be hot,
It is making the iron hot
By striking it.

"Yeats" was correct.

I see my mother's old sad face,
Every night and I wish her
Before I go lay in my bed.

I am never able to look in her eye
And wish her a good night.
She carries too many broken dreams
In her wide white open eyes
Staring me seeking a hug from me.

I avoid hugging her now
It will only make her eyes moist
And break my heart one more time.

What a weak son I am,
Unable to bear her sadness
Helpless to give her any comfort.

When our eyes do meet, they ask:
"Was it worth fighting?"

...and the unanswered question
Lingers on in an empty space between us.

I wish we both knew
How to live
Just for ourselves.

Those days of childhood
I cried
I smiled
I laughed

...the words, the rhythm, the sounds
...the sadness, the happiness, the freedom

Now I know
It was always you alongside me
You my poetry ....! I have found you now.

Words of firmness,
Resolute and full of willpower.

I have always seen you
A character of strength
Living with purpose.

Thank you for being
My mother.

Poetry is like
Dipping the pen
Into the ink of your soul
And writing poems.

You are made of stars.
You are the universe,
You are made of its dust.

From dust to oceans.
From oceans to mother's womb,
From one salt water to another.

Inside is the gushing blood.
Inside your veins is the life,
Outside it drips in your tears.

Live and live again,
You will become dust again.
You are made of stars.
You are the universe,
You are made of its dust. (B.G.)

Life in a bag

Some watch you walk
They learn.
Some watch you fall
They learn.

They all learn,
Some want you to fall
Some pick you up.

The moon
The city
The people.

So many people.....

So many alone
In the cities of structures
Just like the moon.

-B.G.

Life in a bag

The pain never leaves,
It flows with the blood
Under your glowing skin.

The pain never leaves,
With emotional flood
All goes into a spin.

The pain never leaves,
It sits deep into the heart
And the silent Void
Reflects in the eyes
Like an eye of a storm
Quiet, still and faint.

Mending the
Broken heart
Is a task so hard.

With every
Shattered piece
Putting together
Is so hard.

With weight of a
Broken heart
So rigid to try
And move a yard.

Weak and feeling
So exposed
Silently putting
Up your guard.

Discrimination is a
Two-way street.

Then I was taunted
For wearing a turban
And today for
Not wearing one.

Discrimination made me strong
Bigotry bruised me.

I want to write your story
Into the peaks of Himalaya's.

I want your name to echo in air
Passing through high pine trees.

I want to freeze your presence in time
Holding on to you forever and forever.

I want to run through your memories
Like the wind through the rolling valleys.

-B.G.

I wish I was drunk
With love.

Love would give me
Wings to fly away
Escaping the reality
Of brutal boredom.

It will end the
Aimless wandering
Starring into the
Starry night, all alone.

And the wine would
Taste pleasurable,
Night would never end.

Worse luck
I am not drunk on love.
I get by writing poetry.

I begged
To be saved.

My soul was
Soaked
And drenched
In loneliness.

They all walked
Away...
My soul
Screamed
As their footsteps
Faded away.

I die a
Quite
and Silent
Death.

The black
Bag that I carried.
Friends
Asked me once
"What's in this bag?"

These are the
Journals I write,
The literature I bear
The poems I weave
And the stories I tell.

My life shrank
Into a bag,
This is the weight
Of my life
That I carry.

I carry my life
In a bag.

They pumped their chest,
They stared down my eyes.

.... and said:
"You can not battle the storm.
We are the victors."

I was silent
Like silence before the storm.

Tears
Are abandoned words
Rolling down the cheeks
To be seen
To be understood.

I thank all the doors
Which closed on me.
I thank all the obstacles
Which blocked my way.
I thank all my failures
Which became my teachers.

I am thankful, that you
Stoped me from being somewhere
I was not meant to be.

I am thankful, that you
Gave me an opportunity to seek
My true place with true success.

Broken hearts
And
Broken dreams
Can never be renewed.

They never heal,
They never live.

My blood drops
are still warm
Drenching the soil.

My tongue stutters
Narrating the horror
And stories of tears
And depression.

But, I deserve to tell
My story, the story
Of long lonely journey
Of the abandoned people.

I owe it to them.

-B.G.

Life in a bag

Some days
I need a hug.

I settle with
Two shots
Of whisky
And a poem.

-B.G.

Pain is mother of strength
Without pain,
strength is never born.

Accept
The storms
In your life.

You need rain
To grow into
A beautiful flower.

Nothing to fear from the dead,
It is the living who scare me.
Nothing to fear from the change,
It is the fear of no changing coming.

-B.G.

(addicted to love)

Drunk
With love
Flying high
Into the sky.

No wine in World
Can replace the feeling.

No grief
No bitterness
Just the intoxication
And hallucinations.

Addicted to love I am.
I want to stay there,
Hate is too agonizing.

Follow your dreams. Go on a journey.

Healing:

Rest
Recover
Reflection &
Rebound.   —B.G.

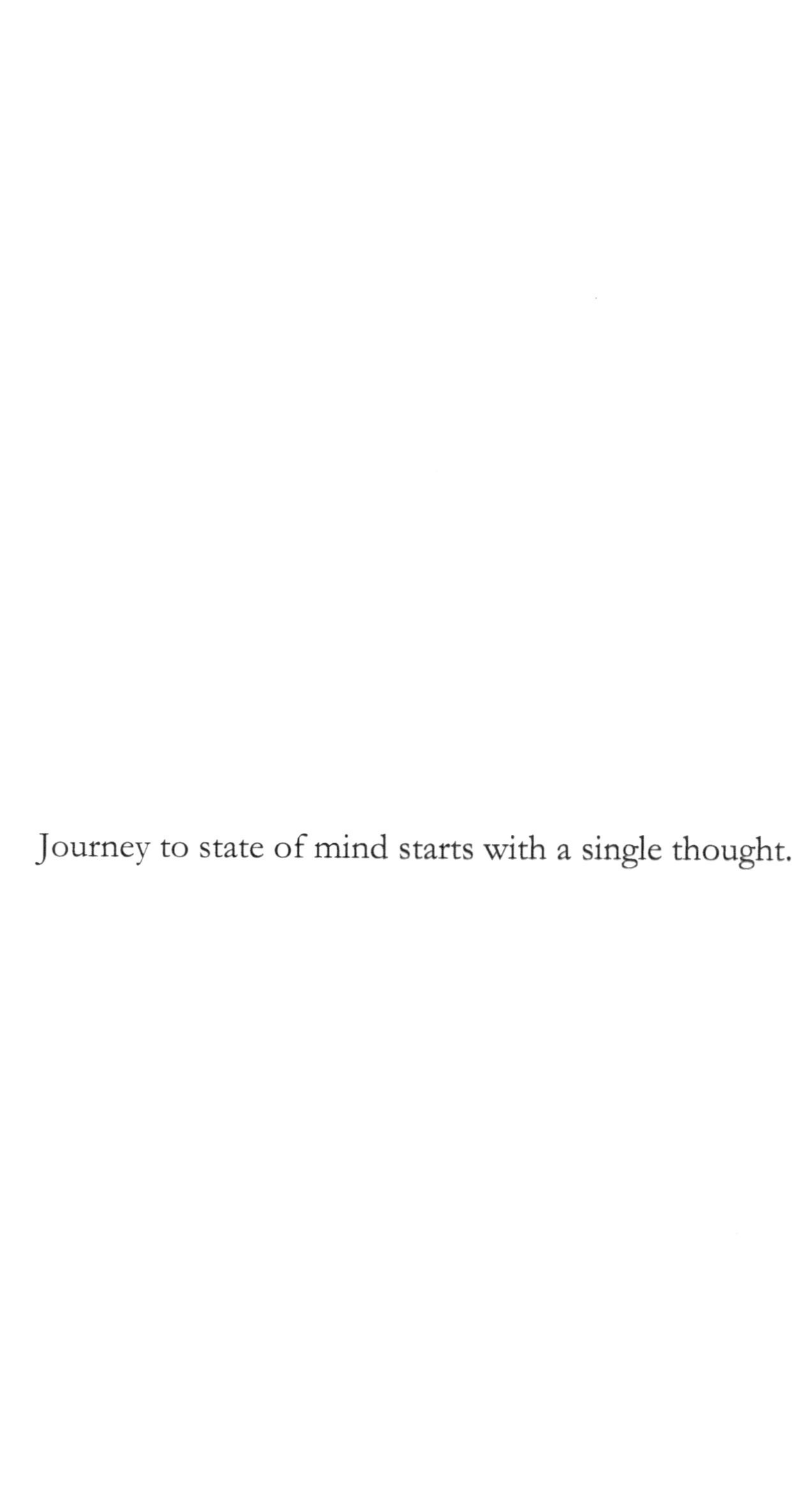

Journey to state of mind starts with a single thought.

When nature dictates, I write.
Trees sing song of winds
Bugs play with leaf
Lamp flickers in
Far away hut
And my poetry
Reaches the tree roots,
Being one with nature.

The deep winter evening.
With last rays of sun,
Hiding away into the horizon.

I miss someone.
A hallow emptiness,
Within.

The sadness,
Of forever losing someone.

The loneliness,
More unbearable then death.
I fear this evening the most.

Have the courage to throw pebble into the still water.

Gobind - The Warrior Saint

With no words to say
I stare across 'sarsa'
Into the foggy jungle,
and I hear your horse
walking through the grass.

You gave your father
Four sons and a mother,
You faced your destiny
And left.

You became a legend
A complete book of history,
My eyes are beautified
Reading it.

From you I learned the importance
Of sacrifice,
Oh, my King, my warrior saint
I feel empty without you holding me.

*sarsa: River flowing through Punjab

I was being hacked and butchered
With sharp words.

The wounds are mostly healed,
But the silence and inactivity of
My associates and confidants
Still haunts me.

I am fragile
Like a flower,
Blown away with wind.

I wanted to be tough
Like truth.
Like her,
Like my sister.

Most times
Be the bigger person
And walk away.

Once in a while
Be the bigger Don
To remind the World
Who it's dealing with.

// BG //

*Scottish meaning of "Don": Great chief

I stopped
Hoping for a light
At the end of the tunnel.

I lit my own candle.

The World would have not known
the fisherman Santiago
if Ernest Hemingway would have
not written "old man and the sea".

Santiago is still alive.

Nothing changes except the faces of the criminal perpetrator and the faces of their victims.

Once upon a time...
Hope was almost fading...
And the heart murmured,
"Give it one more try"

...and that made all the difference.

// BG //

I am changed.

I no longer
Make an effort
To fit into the World.

A soldier,
Paid to fight.
It does not matter
What a soldier thinks,
He must take orders.

A rebel,
Stands for what he believes.
Revolution, Freedom and Love
Is so core of his soul.

Life made me a soldier
Death took me as a rebel.

You been told
You are meek
And silent.

Time comes upon you
When you gather
Every drop of courage,
Look straight into
The eye of your fear.
You have decided to
Fight with such thunder
Breaking the silence
Till the end of time.

Have you seen
Hope dying?
I have seen it,
In my mother's eyes.

\-

I have lived it
Knowing,
I will never be loved.

\-

When all hope dies
It is the saddest
Truth of universe.

\-

Justice is so overrated
Rare it is served,
Either you get it
Or you buy it.

(for J.J. Daly's mother)

Strolling down the hills
Swinging cane in the air
Whistling with the birds
Kicking stones down hills.

Eating plum at chairing cross
Time to go back to barracks
Enjoy some warm Indian food
Salute Officers riding the horse

Soldiers life fighting for Queen
Revolution is calling within me
I am Irelands son walking the hills
This poem is for my mother Queen.

"You were not born to work and pay bills.
You were born to love, enjoy and thrive.

Most importantly you were born to enjoy a
good sleep under the shade of a tree.
Somewhere there if you can fit in writing
poetry, that would be a plus."

[BG]   

When life broke,
It pricked me
Sliced me
And I bled poetry.

(Mutineers of Dagshai)

Crisp fresh breeze
Of Himalayas,
Creasing my skin
Kissing high peaks.

When I stand eyes closed
near the church
On the hill;
The wind whispers
The lost stories of Ireland's
Forgotten sons.

The half-buried graves
Hidden beneath the
Wild mountain grass,
They sleep silently
With bullet holes
And broken bones.
The mutineers
My brothers
You sleep in peace.

My writing
May not be enough
To change the World,
But it's enough
To create ripples
In people's thoughts
Like a skipping stone
Making ripples
Across the still water.

Unconditional love,
I doubt there is
Such a thing.

I believe in it, but
The world continues
To prove me wrong.

And wrong I am.
Tired
Frustrated
And sad.

I am no longer able to
Fulfill the conditions
So that I can too be loved.

It is for the love that we fight
It was for the free life that we fight

Revolutions are not erected in moments,
Revolutions are raised on the graves of generations,
Riding on the train of time.

We refuse to live the way we are forced to live.

Listen! We are here
We are here to stay,
To spark hope,
To ignite the fire of passion
To inspire our generations.

Our children, the children of revolutionaries will live on
fighting you
Inspiring next generations.
We will never give up, be sure of that.

(For James Joseph Daly – Mutineer)

The sound of the soft wind
Taping on my shoulders
And kissing my hairs.
...... I remember,

I felt my mother's gentle touch
I felt her soft kiss on forehead
And then I walk away, dressed
In soldiers uniform holding gun.

...... came so far in Himalayas
Far away for my home land, my
Beautiful Ireland.

My mother waited
And I could never return
I still roam the mountains.

For you my Ireland, I died.

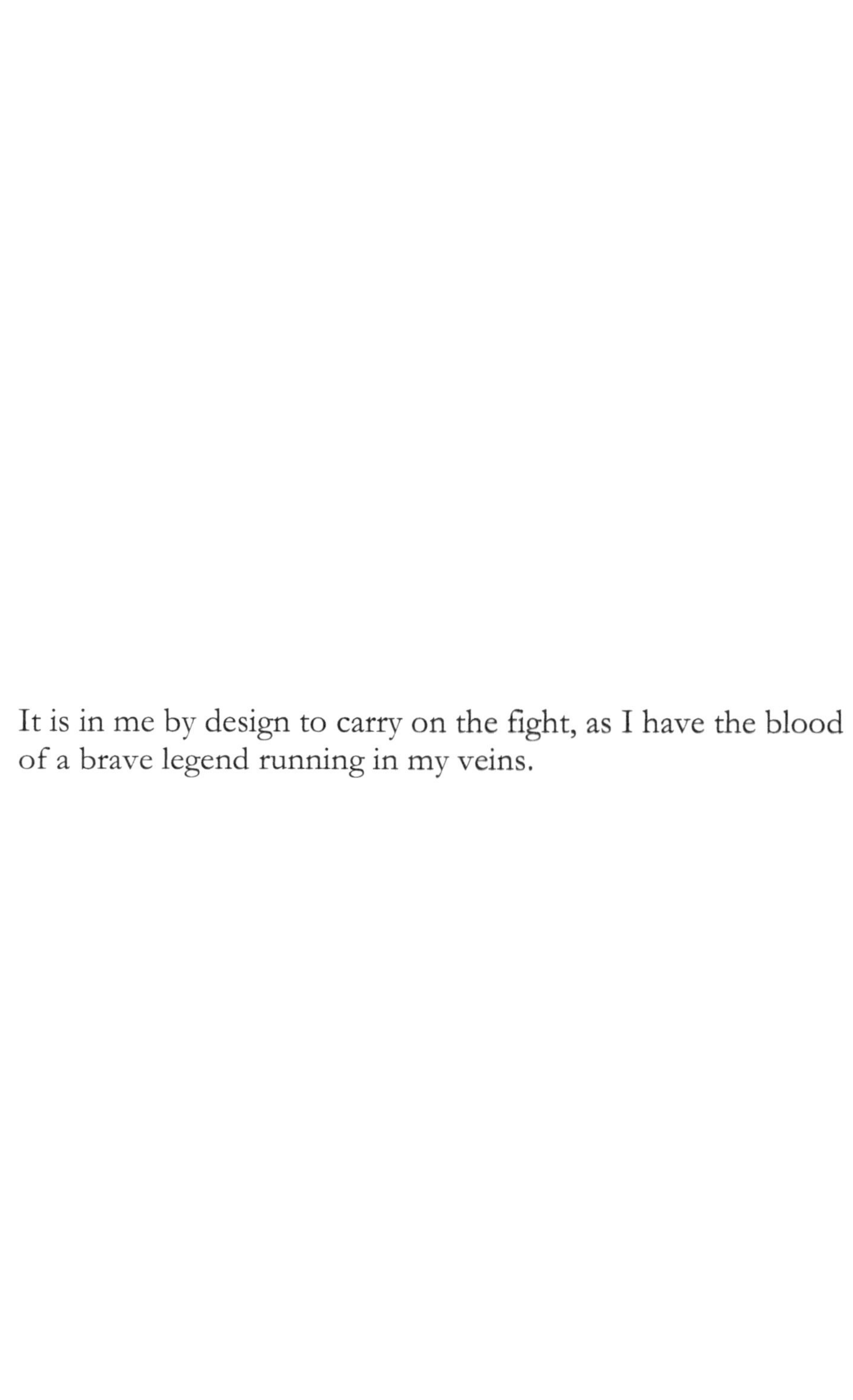

It is in me by design to carry on the fight, as I have the blood of a brave legend running in my veins.

My philosophy always been to try out
different things without the worry of failure
or success, specially the ones which I
suspect I can not achieve. I rather fail
trying than not trying at all. This habit of
mine have given me wonderful
opportunities to experience amazing
things. (B.G.)

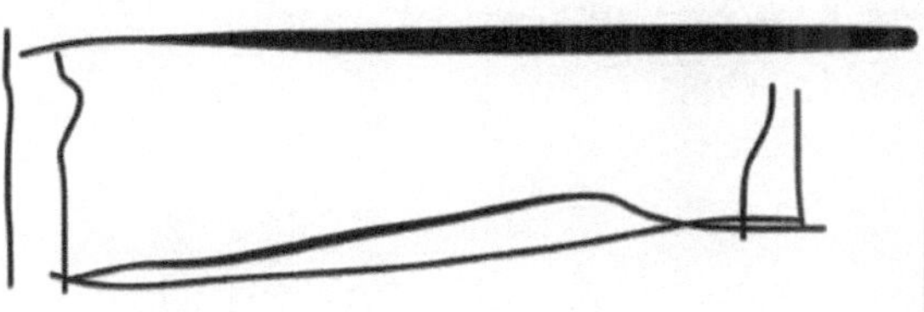

Living in the moments of sadness
is not going to be the way of my life.

It is on me to bring the light of hope.
It is in me to lead and grasp to ever
ray of hope.

It is for me to sow the seed of change.
I am son of fearless fighter who fought for the plight of his
people.

He fought only with his thoughts, his ideas, and choose not
to turn his back to his people.

I am son of a legend.
I must continue to carry the flame
which my father lit.

Blue Star

A blue star
up in the sky.

No, it's the blue light
from the bombs falling
on the golden temple
the Hari's mandir.

The blue light from the eyes
of a dead Sikh child
which have flickered and vanished
thundering and lighting the sky
for a moment,
and will never glow again.

It was the light from the chuni*
of a Sikh woman lying dead
on the walkway
and her blood joining the
ever pure pool of nectar.

On a dark night
sky is filled with blue star's
they are those who vanished
in 1984.

*traditional long scarf worn by south Asian women

For Saffie-Rose Roussos
& many more victims of Manchester

Saffie, like Rose
Beautiful, Innocent
Full of life.

...and plucked away
Before the bloom of spring.

My heart breaks for you,
I have many prayers
And a tear for you.

We will stand defiant
In love with strength
That is the only
True tribute for you.

The depth of the loneliness
Is measured by the silence
Of the evening,
With chatter of friends,
And the count of empty wine glasses.

I am.
I am alive.
I am alive here.

I am alive here;
And that is a miracle.

After the last train have left
After the good byes are done
I will still wait.
Wait is the only hope I would have.

I will sit on the bench
By the station platform.
The rain drop will console me
And, I will wait with eyes closed.

In the crisp cold night
Through the floating fog
I will seek the yellow light of engine
Waiting to hear the horn,
the signal of you coming again.

In the end I realized
Promises are just words,
They can be erased and rewritten.

A bag full of poems
Prose, and books.
This is enough to cherish
For a life time

The poets muse
Sometimes is the pain itself.
The poets muse
Is rarely a beautiful goddess
And when she is,
She had shattered his heart
Into small poems.

Courage sometimes
Shows up holding stone
In a child's hand
Confronting a gun barrel.

...and sometimes, the child
Grows into a poet and writes
A poem saying, "I Protest."

Be Kind. It's Humane.

I Cry Poems.

Broken heart,
Tears, memories
And emotions.

They keep me moving.

Once the heart is broken
It forever becomes a poet.

You need an enlightened mind
To understand the painful heart,
And to feel the wandering soul.

Believing is not knowing.

I no longer believe
in a miracle.
I am the witness
To its existence.

To live
To walk
To leave a mark.

All in a grand moment
Like a stanza of
An epic poem.

Walking down the life
In a Grandeur style
Leaving delicate marks
Of your presence.

That is life my dear friend.

It is so
Easy to wish
But,
So hard to be
A candle.

One must
Burn
To give light.

To find faith
One must surrender
Their own set
Of rules.

Sometimes
Somethings and
Some people never come around.

And that is that.

Making love is sin.
It is to be done hidden,
Away from the
Hostile eyes.

And the
Violent butchery
Is granted
The public legitimacy.

This is the
Horrific love story
Of human kind.

Give your enemy
A fighting chance.

Even enemy
Deserves to
Die with dignity.

Her eyes are pathway
To her tortured soul.

Do you see her story
Reflecting in her tired eyes?
Do you see
A tale of courage,
Survival and determination?

I do.

Today
I lost a piece of me,
Part of my heart
Breathed its last.

A broken heart
No longer beats.
It is no longer longing
For love.

My heart
Understands now,
Not everyone
Is worth loving.

In the end
You will be
Strong and alone.

I rather be alone
Then to have someone,
Who does not
Want to be with me.

I want them in whole, not is pieces.
I want everything or nothing at all.

How long
Can the heart understand.

It will one day
Get disheartened
And tired,
Silently turning away.

The evening
Engulfed in silence.
The shadows vanish
Of the ghostly buildings.

... waiting for the morning sounds
And the human noise, once again.

The season of writing books
while sipping
on a warm cup of tea is here.

The beautiful cold December
Foggy days and sprinkled snow.
I look out the window at children
Making snow man
Wrapped in Christmas lights.

The warm people
Of a cold Nation,
The land of maple leaf.

The best feeling!

We all have our cross that we carry.
We must carry it with faith and courage, just like he did.

I am told I am a poet,
Good to know.

I just express
What I see
What I feel
And what I believe.

I thought I was simply
Expressing life
With harmless words.

I am told they are not words
But, flying bullets capable of
Ripping through the souls.

It's good to know.

Falling apart
Was an enlightening moment.

A painful opportunity
To build myself from the
Broken pieces.

What I made of myself
Is beautiful.

Sometimes you lose,
And that's life.

Sometimes failures are
Far more important
Then victories,
And that's that.

Memories

They are the things of our past
But not forgotten or left behind
We hold them close and tight
In our heart it smites

They are our friends and foe
Tangled in our mind and soul
When loneliness grips at night
They glow with hope and light

Months and years will go by
They make us laugh and cry
These are memories so bright
These are memories so bright

Let go
Of your fears.

Shed off the
Dead weight.

Breathe,
Walk light
Into the new.

Live, love
and dance a little.
You are alive.

Life in a bag

Poem of Valentine

He who was cursed by the fate
He who cannot be loved,
Once said:

Love is love
When caged in a prison.
Love is love
When thrown into
The torture chambers.
It makes saints out of men.

Love when free,
Fly away into the thin air.
Men fall to knees in despair
Who can never be loved again.

Why do people throw stones
Into the water at the beach?
Is it just something to do,
Or they hope stones will float?

The old age
The subtle times.
The last act of life,
Play it well.

Nations are made of people,
religion is people made.
It is the people who fight, kill and massacre.
Nations and Religion are just masks that people hide behind.
Cowards.

        "I don't write to teach anyone, I write to make them think."

Almighty,
Here I stand
In front of you.

You can judge me
As you choose.

I will not give
A single evidence
Of my innocence.

Some days
it's terrifying to be a writer

I am the fire
Of a pyre
Where souls rest
before being
One with the creator.

I am the fire
Of a pyre
Which burns the body
And frees the soul.

Giving
Is beautiful.

Receiving
Is comforting,
Someone cares about you.

I no longer
Go after forcing things.

I let everything flow.
Nothing crashes,
It just comes and go.

Calmness of solitude
Fills my heart and mind,
Nothing is above me or below.

Living in the present does not mean to forget your past. Living in present simply means don't let any unpleasant events of the past ruin your present.

Our past is what makes us who we are today. It is important for us as humans to treasure our past, continue to bloom in our present and dream of our future.

I have always
Honoured my inner child.

He gives me my
Imagination,
My curiosity and
My determination
To try new things in life.

Without him
I will be soulless.

Be friends
With your shadow,
And you will never be alone.

Roar back
At your fears,
And you will never be afraid.

Learn
From your failures,
And you will never be without a teacher.

Turn your pain
Into your art,
And you will never be without love.

Remembrance is my
Sacred obligation.

Remembrance of my history,
Filled with
Fear
Loss
Torture
Death
And stolen childhood.

Remembrance of those times
Of Sikh Genocide, the brutality
Of my fellow human kind.

I remember
With my bruised soul
And a broken heart.

I remember those
Who no longer walk the earth
They only live in memories.

I cry along with those
Who are reminisces of the ruins.

My history is my legacy,
My words is all I can give
To my generations to come.

My words are my efforts
To rise from the ruins,
To rise above the hate.

Life in a bag

They
Came into my house
Making noises of
heavy army boots.

They pointed a pistol
At me;
I did not close my eyes.

They killed many
In cold blood.

They created the
Most dangerous rebel,
They created a writer.

Writing purifies my thoughts and my soul. It is like the river Ganges, it cleanses me of my sins.

My scars
Are nothing more than
A reminder,
That the life tried to break me down
And it failed.

Laugh till
It hurts.
Start writing
When it hurts.

Write passionately
About your laughter
And your pain.

Writing to me is living the moments again, tasting life the
second time.

Someday,
When I am gone.
Someone will read
My soul on the pages
Of my book.

And I will live again.

They pushed me
Into the water,
Thinking I will drown.
Instead, I learned to swim.

They left me
To the wolves,
Thinking I will be butchered.
Instead, I lead the pack.

They threw me
Into the fire,
Thinking I will burn to ashes.
Instead, I become the Sun.

Giving up
Is not
Part of my DNA.

By design
I have no choice,
I fight till the end.

Poetry
Is the echo
Of my mind,

You are my greatest creation
You remind me of my existence,
My act of being God.

All creations must ruin,
That is the law of nature.

To lose you is what I fear the most,
You are also my greatest sorrow.
Even the Gods agonize and suffer.

Some people
Are beyond words,
You are one of them.

Once you accept yourself
For who you are,
That's when the journey starts.

The ruins
Of my life
Once gave me
The best moments,

And now they give me
The Best memories.

Don't fit
Into a box.

Be the air,
The water
And flow.

Artists are the most powerful and effective rebels and
that is why the oppressive regime's fear them the
most.

Once upon a time
Moon was my friend.

The dream would fly
Across the blue sky

Once upon a time
Trees played with me.

Our shadows never left us
Loneliness was far from us

Time flew away, and the friends
Loneliness embraces all.

Life in a bag

Mostly fiction is truth wrapped in covers of the imagination.

The wind
Knows me.

It understands
We both are same,
Whirling dust and storm.

I tried.
I did try to look away
Like a coward, but
Fragments of honour and pride
In my blood
Did not let me.

Best way to heal,
Is to get
Intimate with your
Pain, with your wounds and
With your tears.

FROM THE AUTHOR

"There are no rules to writing. I simply write. I write for myself. I write about what I know and about my experiences, this way I can be passionate about what I write. Being passionate about my writing is important to me.

-b.g.

www.ingramcontent.com/pod-product-compliance
Lightning Source LLC
Chambersburg PA
CBHW031339060726
47590CB00007B/2536